# Cycles of love

First published in Great Britain, 2023



Printed and bound in Great Britain by Ramona Ashby.

For Dante

# I went round and round, through the cycles of love

Ramona Ashby

# Contents

# CELEBRATION

# Sweet nectar

On a natural high,
I dance,
flutter
like the essence of a hummingbird,
soaring to the nectar of a rose –
its resurgence.

I hold you dearly, embracing your warmth,
elated.

Eye to eye.

Your hand on my curve, we sway.

Our bodies, pulsating, receptive
to the other,
whining to the beat;
enjoying this unison.

We succumb,
addicted.

The joy is felt.

Hearts strumming a symphony,
slow motions of ecstasy,
as we dance.

We're addicted.

# Naked souls

You came.

We conversed our wants,
dreams.

Undressed wounds,
of yesteryear,
childhood tales of us.

With fondness we laughed,
reconnecting,
reminiscing on memories of our friendship.

Separated by distance,
yet no resistance to try.

You charmed me with your playfulness and
warmth.

Facing a desire to learn more,
we communicated tirelessly
baring our souls.

# Beautiful

Sweet harmony in your eyes.

Your amorous words saturate my every sense.

I'm excited, trusting in your every
promise.

I'm in a rapture of you.
With every heartbeat, my mind says,
this is beautiful.

I'm weak at the knees.

Your being, renders me
speechless.

Like the allure of a chocolate truffle
every layer, I unpeel to
reveal, every inch of me –
I feel,
beautiful.

I've not known,
I've not felt
like this.

It is
simply,
beautiful.

# Cloud nine

Before I lay my head to sleep,
I asked.
By day
I received.
You.

Along you came, adorable and true.
I celebrate getting to know you.
This is exciting, enchanting.
Intentions long-lasting.
I've been saving for someone special.

A destination,
you've never known.

On a spiritual journey that is fulfilling of
mind, body and soul.

Let me take you to
cloud nine.

I'll treat you so
good.

Love you so
good.

I am on
cloud nine.

# Check!

Reality
check.

I look at you,
you at me.

A connection.

Promises, effort and action.

Check!

Soulful, a divine attraction,
satisfaction
I will hold.

Are you where you want to be?!
No sitting under my apple tree!

No sampling, using
nor playing with my heart!

I declare.

Be a nourishing love.
You pour and I pour –
we are a family.

Check!

My spirit is level.

# Cocoa butter

Soothing,
melting in my silky skin.

Cocoa brown, cocoa rich,
the aroma of caramel.

I glow, as you perform.

Taking me high,
infusing my inner.

Languishing in,
we caressing in,
cocoa butter.

You a taste of the exotic:
creamy,
nutty, sweet.

I savour you.

You on me, delightful,
I gush, as you
engulf my nakedness.

Again, and over again
cocoa butter, me,
again.

# Footsteps of love

With every step,
I love
with every breath,
I love
with every tear,
I love
with every action,
I love
with every fall,
I love
with every tantrum,
I love.
In every way,
I love.
'til my last step,
I will love you.

# ECSTASY

# The sensation

I breathe
I hear
I see you.

I feel
I touch
I stroke you.

I want
I need
I yearn
I desire you.

I seek.
I love only you.

# Paradise connection

Clear blue skies,
oh the beauty in you.
A radiating sun,
expressing a calm,
balancing of the soul.

Coconut trees lean majestically like a king over his queen.
Beach grapes trail,
ripe,
precious juice to quench.
Jagged cliffs,
lashed by nature's work, an art form.

The rush of waves strumming a peaceful symphony – streaming to our feet.
I love this, you and I,
rolling on top o'er each other,
rhythmically on caramel grains.

Glistening dark skins,
kinked hair waving,
rippled backs of strength writhing.
Manifestation of our fantasy, I'm riveted by you.

Tongues lashing, moistening of my fruit, groans of pleasure.
Our union, crossing to a new level.
Long-distance love with emotions,
words, feeding our hearts,
we are open, love floods.

We perspire,
an intensity of heat,
a climaxing of our bodies.
This freedom
is ours;
love is ours.
We're in paradise.

# Legacy of love

Summer heat!
I cooked your favourite –
stew chicken and rice;
rum punch; lots of ice.
You say,
delicious,
I say,
my love potion.

You come behind me,
breathing on
the nape of my neck.
Takes my breath away.
I gasp, then laugh,
I'm glowing.
Cheeks together, you take a snap
capturing our
contentment.

Sentiments of 90s RnB,
sounding so nice.
I'm almost weak.
I tease and dance –
I think you're hypnotised.
Your eyes follow,
admire,
appreciate,
I feel you grow.

A sweet breeze through the back door.
Moderating the fire we make.
We on a mission,
bodies aligned.

You're caressing my hair, head in motion;
your hands on my hips pulling me in
deep.

Our eyes locking intermittently,
our skins shimmering;
I'm rocking with glee.
Vocalising approval.

Scented candles, steady;
silhouettes on the floor,
sharing rounds of pleasure
through till night.

# Pepper sauce

I know my baby loves me,
the way that he holds,
the way he caresses me.

Kiss me on my nipple,
slip to my middle,
mek me dribble.

Taste my lips, taste my flavour – savour that pleasure.
Ecstasy is pouring, my mind is soaring.

I trickle my sweetness on your face.

You dip that throne,
inch by inch and strong, through
my endless valley.

Over and over, you take me on this journey.

A no return destination – pleasure.
As I scream your name, you flow,
as you tell me I am yours.
Forever.

# Bended knee

That day,
your plea to me,
down on bended knee.

I surrendered to you.

With gushing tears, love and affection.
I embraced your question.

And said yes.

Yes, a promise of love,
to be your wife,
together for life.

# REALISATION

# Bittersweet

You gave me candy then snatched it back.
Just like that.

I was blindsided,
you didn't care.
Thought you were sweet,
kind and neat.

Your curses;
betrayal,
laid for all to see.
You were playin' me.

I held on,
flashes of hope.
Commitment was dear to me.

You, this girl and the next.
Tears fell; as I bled inside.
You, running around town with many.

You turned and walked away.
I don't like what I see,
yet fond of the good memories
I questioned,
but you refuse –
now my back is to you.
I never really knew you.

I invested too soon.
Sowed seeds of hope.

I offered.

Took me for my good nature.
'twas bittersweet.

# Dear me

Why ya don't listen?!
Ya think he wants you?!
Ya think he loves you?!
He's been tellin' you, many have been tellin' you.
Wolf in sheep clothin' they call him!
Yet ya choose to accept his bad treatment.
Then he says he loves you,
playin' mind games with you.
Look,
there's no effort.

Ya heart hurtin' – feels there's no care.
It's only you who loyal!
It's only you who made yourself clear.

Ya better listen to
ya intuition.

It gine hurt to accept the truth.
It gine take a long time to get over.
But, it's for the best!
Ya been served protection by his rejection.
Wha' kinda man act so like that?
His actions been disgraceful!
Now it's time to close the door in his face,
mek him lose you,
don't let him abuse you!

# Dear X

I shoulda listened,
you said we were through.

Shoulda heard that you were doin you.

Now I'm breakin my own heart,
utilising energy saying I love you,
at times –
I hate that, I hate you!

The pangs of pain, anxiety.

I'm breakin down.
Shit, this is bullshit!

I hear you.

We are through.

I hear you are sorry.

Boy, this is my story!

I take that step forward,
being true to myself
and loving me for all the glory.

This is goodbye.

# The cry

The cry of a man,
from the depth of his belly
he howls.
Head bowed.

A man who's ego
has been stroked.
Pacifying gains;
lashes of lust,
he thrusts,
fast and furious;
bodies,
not loving minds.
Rounds of pleasure,
feeding his masculine desire.
Societal practices;
feeding his
promiscuity.

The cry,
for his father's guidance,
to quell the hurt,
he passes woman to
woman.
His emotions restless.

The cry of a man,
who is lost,
a seeker,
needing redemption
of this infidel cycle.

The cry of his daughter,
shamed by her father;
grandfather;
supposed models of men.
She loves them,
yet,
hates their cycle,
of love.

The cry of a woman.

# Her cycle

I look at myself.
Senses say, love feels good,
what is said sounds good,
wait, just wait and see.

Loneliness, loss –
my traps of misery.

I try again.

I don't want to lose this fight for love.

But I'm losing myself.

Nothing deep to see here!
A mirror reflects our cracked souls,
a vacancy for satisfaction.

On this dating field,
I'm
chasing, kicking,
rolling stones like daddy,
flaws uncanny.

Oh dad if you only knew,
how much your daughter goes through!

I quit the game.

I choose to break the cycle.

# BREATHE OUT

# Broken

When the night is still,
broken souls,
I hear you cry,
you won't die.

Hear me –
pull back.

All the trust that you gave – pull back
And forgive.

You.

Give it all right back,
to yourself.

You will be alright.

# Solitude

Appreciating.
And accepting me.

Here I sit, looking
in the mirror.

I am responsible for the reflection.

I am responsible for my experience.

Smiling, in the stillness of a solitary life.

It is alright to be me, alright to admire me.

I am complete, in my own presence.

# Replenish

Take me.

For I have been in the desert;
with my tears.

I'm alone.

I'm in pain.

God are you there?!
Replenish me.

Take my mistrust,
my anger,
my vengeance;
use me as a resource.

I come to you – asking for strength.

I come to you,
love is my gift.

I come to you,
wisdom
to offer.

I come to you,
worthy of the very best.

I am here,
acknowledging me.

Replenish me.

# Reflection

I bought a gold mirror, as
tall as me.

I could see every nook,
and cranny.

I pouted and posed,
dipped low – as far as I could go.

Trailed my hand over my curves,
appreciating my beauty.

I caught myself.

I said it aloud,
I am proud
of me.

The self-love journey,
led to me being free.

My mind is unburdened.

My body an expression,
of the concept
of me.

# Healing

I spend time alone.
I don't pick up my phone
collecting my thoughts –
here they come
running at me,
me
running from them.

My sense, senses
the aroma of incense – Palo Santo, flaring, subtle sweet smells.
I am present.

I choose –
shea butter, to lather my skin,
enriching richness of Africa on me.
The decadence of moringa,
mists my,
neck and wrists.
I am present.

I focus on my breath,
centre myself –
not a perfectly personified woman; I am me.
I flex, I tilt my achy neck, pinching pink quartz earrings, against my dark choco skin.
I smile, at my blackness with pride.
I am present.

My strides, steady and silent.
A reggae rhythm ruptures!
Effortlessly my hips sway,
bouncing glutes collide.
I prance,
two fingers in the air!
My heart picks up a
beat
as I am skankin' sweet.

I sit, to sip, on cerassie tea,
bitter;
yet soothing and cleansing.
The last gulp.
I appreciate its harmony.

My long skirt sculpts me.
Strong cotton, saturates me.
I trail my hand, feeling it's ribbed texture.
A flash of the toil of
mum's mamma –
and ma –
generational woes echoes;
I wipe my brow.
I run from the thoughts
running at me,
me running from them.
I struggle to stay present.

My mouth meets a mango.
My teeth and tongue tango
with its juice;
its sweetness, invites me to tear its layers.
Chewing,
its yellowy,
fleshy,
texture.

Tasting so good.
I
lose
myself.
My face is a mess,
juice dripping on my hands.
I don't mind.
I glide the seed in my mouth, sucking it bare.
I am free.
I am
present.

# Real

My level is intensive.
Highly concentrated, a divine love.
A realist; leaving dreamers to drift on by.

This here is revealing –
let me see all you claim to be:
a man of integrity, honesty.

I need you to show me
you are real.

My vocals soft and steady.
An eloquent melody for wandering ears.
My words simplistic and true.

I address you and you.
Maybe to teach.

Oval eyes, open, reach out to you.

My heart, oh she is healing,
aligned with my head.

My smile is endless.
See my face.

# Meet me in the middle

To my left, to my right,
is space.

Still, I carry myself with grace.
Knowing that I am at peace.

This is serenity,
a space of living and loving me.

Acknowledging my thoughts;
rejecting all that's ill-suited.

My poise is focused.
I voice passion but trust only action.

You're most welcome – if you meet me in the middle.

Somewhere out there,
you are looking for me.

To hold, to love
unconditionally.

A warm welcome!

Serving goodness without measure.

There is gratitude,
when you meet me in the middle.

# Union

There's a union
of head and heart.

Finally, I'm certain
of who I am,
where I want to be.

Self-reflection is my
master, elevating
over yesterday,
yester-year.

Today, rocking
authenticity,
in my smile
and spirit.

# Ramona Ashby

A debut author and poet living in London, born in Barbados. She studied 'Literary studies in English' BA, at University of Bedfordshire.

Poetry has been an outlet since her teens, having been raised in a culture of being 'seen not heard' – "what I couldn't vocalise comfortably, I wrote".

"It's important my writing is relatable and spirited – attributing dialect to capture the essence of my Bajan heritage.

"As a writer, I am no longer constrained."

Instagram: **@blacpoesia**